Chauncey Cheese
GOES ROUND THE WORLD

Vincent Maggio

Illustrations by
Jeff Moores

"For more Cheesy fun" Visit www.chaunceycheese.com Enjoy!

Visit www.booksurge.com to order additional copies.

*To my wife Karen,
my son Vinny, and
my daughter Angela*

One dark and rainy day in a little town known as Lactose, Wisconsin lived a little boy named Billy.

There he sat at the kitchen table staring out the window, counting the rain drops on the window pane, wearing a frown.

Billy's mom took notice of her sad faced son.

"Billy boy, what's wrong?" she asked.

"Mom," said Billy, "I've got nothing to do."

"Why don't you call your friend Vinny across the street and invite him over to play?"

"I did call Vinny," Billy sighed, "and no one is home," Billy's frown grew.

Billy's mom had a great idea; "Billy," she asked, "how would you like a cheese sandwich with a glass of milk?"

That's Billy's favorite lunch, and his frown slowly turned upside down. "Okay Mom, I mean, yes please mommy!"

Billy's mom placed the sandwich and glass of milk in front of him on the kitchen table. "Here you go big guy, enjoy!"

Billy was just about to take his first bite when
all of a sudden, his sandwich began to move.
He jumped back. It was the slice of cheese;
it began to wiggle itself out of his sandwich.

Billy looked on in amazement as the piece
of cheese wiggled out from between the bread,
jumped up onto the rim of his glass of milk
and said…

"Hello Billy boy, my name is Chauncey, Chauncey Cheese…" Billy could barely speak. "Ha ha hello Chauncey."

"How would you like to come with me to meet some of my friends?" Chauncey asked.

"Sure," Billy replied, "Where do they live?"

"Around the world Billy, all around the world."

Chauncey began to grow,

bigger

and bigger

and bigger

until he was the size of Billy's bed spread, which was
yellow too, just like Chauncey.

"Open the window Billy. Hop on my back and hold on tight." Chauncey and Billy were about to set off on a great adventure. Chauncey could fly way up high in the now blue sky.

"Wow Chauncey, you're like a magic carpet."

That's right Billy boy, now hold on tight." Chauncey and Billy flew out of sight.

"Where are we going?" asked Billy.

"First stop will be the beautiful land of Italy.
I want you to meet one of my closest friends,
Mr. Mozzarella, Mario Mozzarella. Do you like
pizza Billy?"

"Oh yes Chauncey, yes I do."

"Then you'll love my friend Mario."

Chauncey picked up speed, flying faster and faster.
"There it is Billy boy. Look, look down there. It's Italy!
Now hold on my friend; it's time to gently touch
down, I can't wait to see my dear friend, Mario!"

Chauncey made a perfect landing. "What's that?"
Billy asked Chauncey.

"Why, that is where Mr. Mozzarella lives, the leaning
tower of Pisa. Go ahead Billy don't be shy, knock on
the door, man, I'm sure he's home."

17

"Chauncey, my pie's on, how are you? Who is this handsome boy?"

"Mario, I would like you to meet my friend Billy."

"Hello Mr. Mozzarella," Billy said.

"Hello Billy, any friend of Chauncey's is a friend of mine."

"So tell me Chauncey," asked Mario, "where else are you going today?"

"Next stop, Switzerland."

"Are you going to visit Suzy?"

"Yes," Chauncey replied, "our beloved friend, Suzy Swiss."

"Can I come too?" asked Mario. "It's been ages since I've seen Suzy."

"Of course you may join us; hop on guys and hold on tight."

19

"Up, up and away we go, off to the land of Swiss, Switzerland!" Within no time they began their descent. "Billy, look down there. Have you ever seen such tall and beautiful mountains?"

"Wow-wee! No I have not, what are they called?" he asked.

"They are the Swiss Alps, that's were Suzy lives. Hold tight my friends and get ready to touch down."

"There she is!" shouted Mario. Look guys there on the mountain top, it's Suzy! Hold tight off we go!"

"Chauncey, Mario, hello hello, it's so nice to see you both, and who is this cute young man?"

"My name is Billy."

"Welcome to my home, Billy, welcome."

"How have you been Chauncey, and you Mario?" Suzy asked.

"We're just grate Suzy, and you?"

"Very well thank you."

"How do you stay so thin," asked Mario.

"Suzy, would you like to come with us to visit with Bobby?"

"I would love to Chauncey, I would love to."

"All right everybody you know the routine, hop on and hold on tight!" Billy shouted.

"That is right Billy, you're catching on. Up, up and away we go, next stop the wonderful country of France."

"Billy, can you see that tall tower in the distance? That is the world famous Eiffel Tower and the home of Bobby Brie, explained Suzy. "Another perfect landing my friends. You are quite the air craft, Chauncey."

"Why thank you, Suzy."

"Chauncey, Mario, Suzy, hello, hello!"

"Greetings Bobby, we would like you to meet our friend Billy, he is from America."

"Hello Billy!"

"Pleased to meet you, Mr. Brie," Said Billy.

"Wow you're from America?"

"Yes Mr. Brie," Billy replied.

"I've always wanted to see the land of the free, the home of the brave," Bobby said. "What do you say Chauncey, can we all go?"

"Of course, but we can't forget Aristotle. You well know how delicate he can be. If he knew that we were all together and did not drop in for a visit, he would crumble."

"Up, up and away, Billy. One last stop before we go home."

"Where to Chauncey?"

"Ancient Greece, we must pick up Aristotle, Aristotle Feta."

"Wow, what's that down there?" Billy asked.

"That is Greece's ancient ruins, the home of ancient Aristotle."

"Careful Chauncey," Suzy uttered, "you know how tender Aris can be, he considers himself to be well-aged."

31

"Chauncey, Mario, Suzan, Robert, it has been quite some time since I've seen all of you. Whom may I ask is this young gentleman?" asked Aristotle.

"My name is Billy. Pleasure to meet you, sir. Mr. Feta, would you care to join us? It's getting late and I have to get back to my house."

"By all means, William, by all means."

"All together now, up, up, and away!" Cried Chauncey. Higher and higher they flew.

"Not too close to the sun," Aristotle warned Chauncey. Again Aristotle spoke, "behold the power of cheese!"

"Faster Chauncey, it's getting late and I don't want my mom to worry." So faster they flew.

"Hey everybody, look down there. That is where I live, that is Lactose Wisconsin! 123 Brickstone Avenue Chauncey."

"Don't worry Billy; I know just which cottage you live in."

"Look Chauncey, the kitchen window is still open."

"Hold on tight everyone, here we go." Into the kitchen window they went.

"Mom, Mom, come quick. I want you to meet all my new friends."

"Mommy, I would like you to meet Chauncey Cheese. He too is from America. This is Mario Mozzarella and he is from Italy. This is Suzy Swiss, she's from Switzerland. This is Bobby Brie, he is from France. And last, but certainly not least, is Aristotle Feta, he is from Greece."

"Well Billy, I was wondering what you were day dreaming about as you looked out the window. You have quite the imagination."

"Mom could you do me a big favor? Can you get the camera and take a picture with me and all of my new found friends?"

Billy's mom laughed, "sure Billy." Everyone gathered around the kitchen table. "Okay get ready everyone, smile and say, **CHEESE**!"

THE END

VINCENT MAGGIO

Vince was born on September 13th, 1960 in New York. He was raised on Long Island in a modest home with his Mother Georgette, Father Vincent, and three sisters Gayle, Cindy, and Lynne. He graduated high school in 1979, at which time he began working various jobs. Vince graduated from SUNY Farmingdale in 1985, while in college he started a small business. His work now brought him to many different homes, while at work he found himself surrounded by naturally inquisitive children. Vince was always answering their questions one after another, after another. It was his turn to start asking questions of his own. He started asking the kid's many different questions as he found their answers quite amusing. One question he would always ask was, do you kid's like cheese? Their initial answer usually was yuck, no way, ah gross. Then he would ask if they liked pizza, well, do you guy's like pizza, oh yes we love pizza, what about macaroni and cheese, ummmmmmm yes we love that too! Apparently most kid's love cheese, Chauncey was born! Vince still lives on Long Island, with his wife Karen, son Mini Vinny, and daughter Angela.

Made in the USA
Charleston, SC
09 June 2011